SECOND CHANCE CHRISTMAS

A True Story

BY JANET DEFEVER

ILLUSTRATIONS BY TAJIN ROBLES

MISSION POINT PRESS

Readers are encouraged to go to MissionPointPress.com to contact the author or to
find information on how to buy this book in bulk at a discounted rate.

Published by Mission Point Press
2554 Chandler Rd.
Traverse City, MI 49696
(231) 421-9513
MissionPointPress.com

Hardcover: 978-1-958363-33-1
Softcover: 978-1-958363-34-8
Library of Congress Control Number: 2022917654

Printed in the United States of America

To Frank, Justine, and Landon —
my constant sources of encouragement

and

To Kristie Kathryn Hancock,
for seeing the intrinsic worth
of a simple childhood story

CHRISTMAS OF 1971 was the year that I learned
three important things about Santa Claus.

First, Santa is always watching at the worst
possible moment.

Second, Santa realizes that no one is perfect.

And third, Santa knows that the most important things
in this world are the things that you cannot see.

I grew up on a small dairy farm in the middle of Michigan.
My earliest memories are of cows, calves, sheep,
chickens, pigs, dogs, and cats. And lots of animals
meant lots of work!

I was eleven years old that Christmas, and I had more
responsibility than most kids I knew. I had to carry the
pails of milk from the barn to the milk house. I had to

walk through manure to spread bales of straw in the new barn where the cows slept at night. I had to fill buckets with grain for the cows to eat while they were being milked. And I had to run from my older brother who liked to punch me in the arm whenever my dad wasn't looking.

My younger sister was seven that year, and she only had two jobs. She had to pour milk in the pan for the cats and bottle-feed the baby calves.

There were four small pens in the back corner of the barn, and it was the only place in our barn where you couldn't see your own breath. Sacks of oats were stacked in the first pen, and we knew that mice were waiting to jump and run over our boots the minute we turned on the light. A bare lightbulb dangled overhead from a black electrical wire, and it lit up every corner of the space with yellow light, making it feel warm and cozy. It was my favorite place on our farm in the winter.

Sometimes between carrying pails of milk, I would run back to see the calves and we would let them suck on our fingers while they waited for their turn at the bottle. We looked for special markings on each calf so we could tell them apart. Every calf had huge brown eyes and long eyelashes, and if you weren't paying attention, it was easy to accidentally give one calf two bottles of milk and then another calf would go hungry all night. They always made us laugh as they pushed each other out of the way to be first, and I could hear my sister giggling at them as I stomped around the barn doing my own chores. Even though she was four years younger than me, it did not seem fair that she had all the fun jobs and I had all the hard jobs! I wanted to be like my friends who lived in town. They didn't have chores to do. They got to stay after school for sports, cheerleading, and Girl Scouts. My mom told me those were things for the town kids; we had work to do.

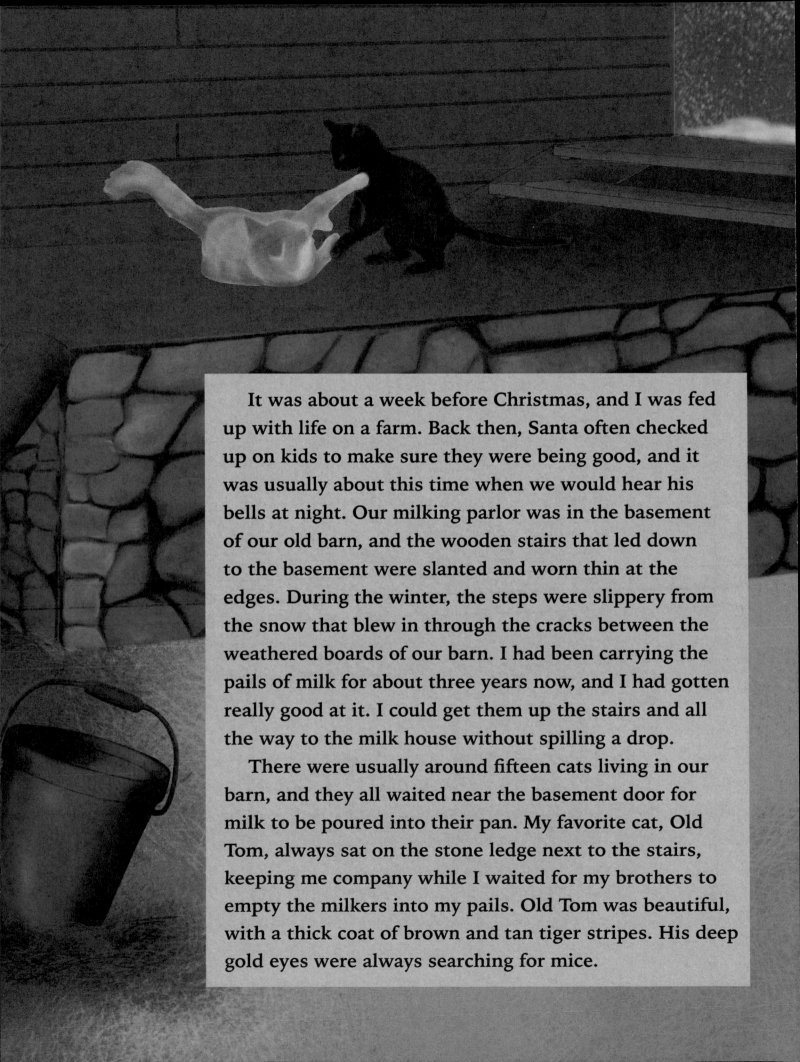

It was about a week before Christmas, and I was fed up with life on a farm. Back then, Santa often checked up on kids to make sure they were being good, and it was usually about this time when we would hear his bells at night. Our milking parlor was in the basement of our old barn, and the wooden stairs that led down to the basement were slanted and worn thin at the edges. During the winter, the steps were slippery from the snow that blew in through the cracks between the weathered boards of our barn. I had been carrying the pails of milk for about three years now, and I had gotten really good at it. I could get them up the stairs and all the way to the milk house without spilling a drop.

There were usually around fifteen cats living in our barn, and they all waited near the basement door for milk to be poured into their pan. My favorite cat, Old Tom, always sat on the stone ledge next to the stairs, keeping me company while I waited for my brothers to empty the milkers into my pails. Old Tom was beautiful, with a thick coat of brown and tan tiger stripes. His deep gold eyes were always searching for mice.

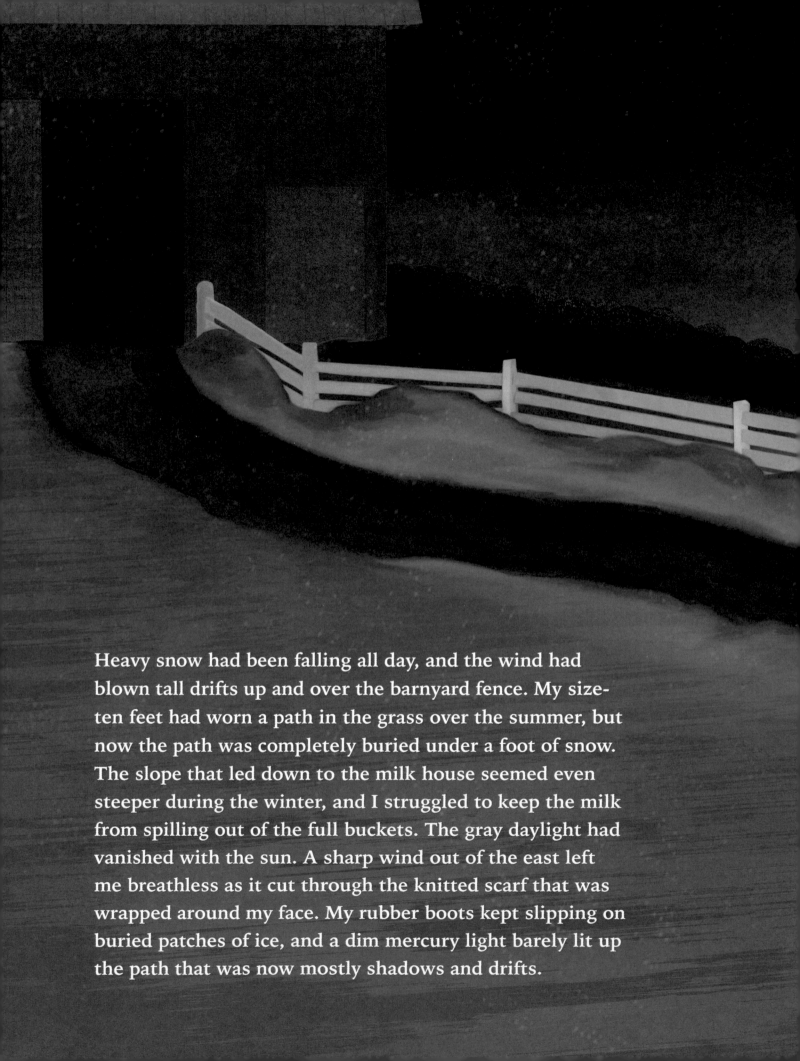

Heavy snow had been falling all day, and the wind had
blown tall drifts up and over the barnyard fence. My size-
ten feet had worn a path in the grass over the summer, but
now the path was completely buried under a foot of snow.
The slope that led down to the milk house seemed even
steeper during the winter, and I struggled to keep the milk
from spilling out of the full buckets. The gray daylight had
vanished with the sun. A sharp wind out of the east left
me breathless as it cut through the knitted scarf that was
wrapped around my face. My rubber boots kept slipping on
buried patches of ice, and a dim mercury light barely lit up
the path that was now mostly shadows and drifts.

I had just come in from the barn, and I was tired and mad. Supper was ready, and I flopped into my chair at the end of the table. My mom had made my favorite meal, chicken and dumplings, and I ate every last bite on my plate. After dinner, all of us kids headed to the living room to watch TV.

But before the picture on the television had even come
into focus, my mom came in and said,
   "Girls, I'm really tired. Will you both come and do
the dishes?"
   My brothers just sat there as we walked back out to
the kitchen. Now I was furious!

I stomped to the sink and pointed my finger at my little sister. *"I'm* washing and *you're* drying!"

She pointed her finger right back in my face and said, "No! *I'm* washing and *you're* drying!"

What came next was a flurry of hateful words and screaming. We slapped each other as hard as we could with our dish towels and shoved each other until my sister fell into the pile of dishes that was stacked on the counter.

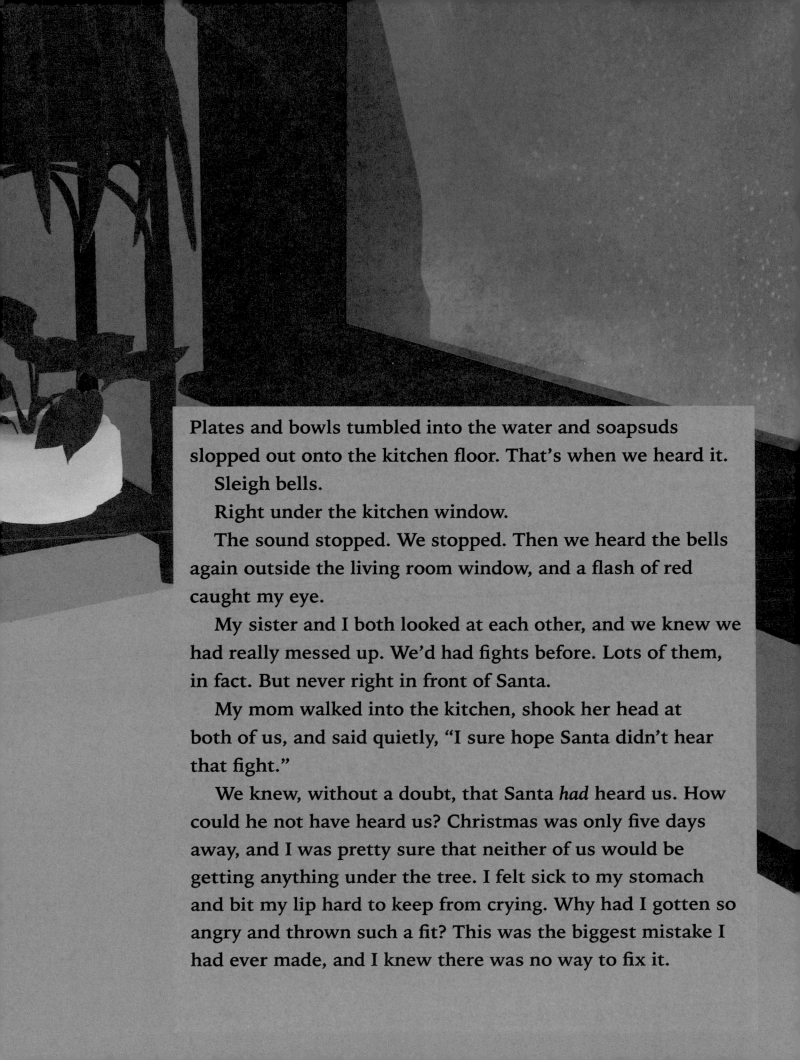

Plates and bowls tumbled into the water and soapsuds slopped out onto the kitchen floor. That's when we heard it.

Sleigh bells.

Right under the kitchen window.

The sound stopped. We stopped. Then we heard the bells again outside the living room window, and a flash of red caught my eye.

My sister and I both looked at each other, and we knew we had really messed up. We'd had fights before. Lots of them, in fact. But never right in front of Santa.

My mom walked into the kitchen, shook her head at both of us, and said quietly, "I sure hope Santa didn't hear that fight."

We knew, without a doubt, that Santa *had* heard us. How could he not have heard us? Christmas was only five days away, and I was pretty sure that neither of us would be getting anything under the tree. I felt sick to my stomach and bit my lip hard to keep from crying. Why had I gotten so angry and thrown such a fit? This was the biggest mistake I had ever made, and I knew there was no way to fix it.

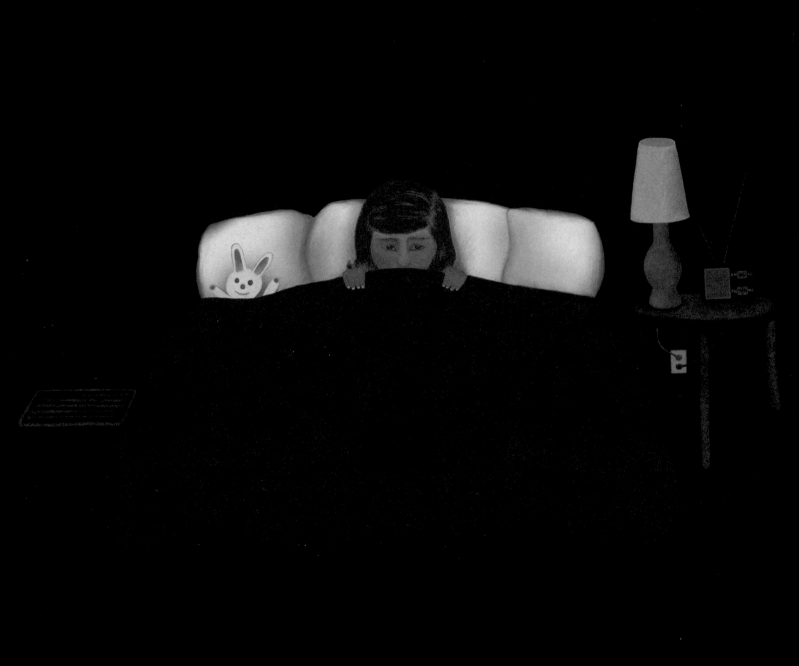

For the next few nights, I did my chores and helped out around the house as much as I could. So did my sister. We knew there was no way to change what had happened, but I think we were both hoping that somehow, in some way, we could make things right again.

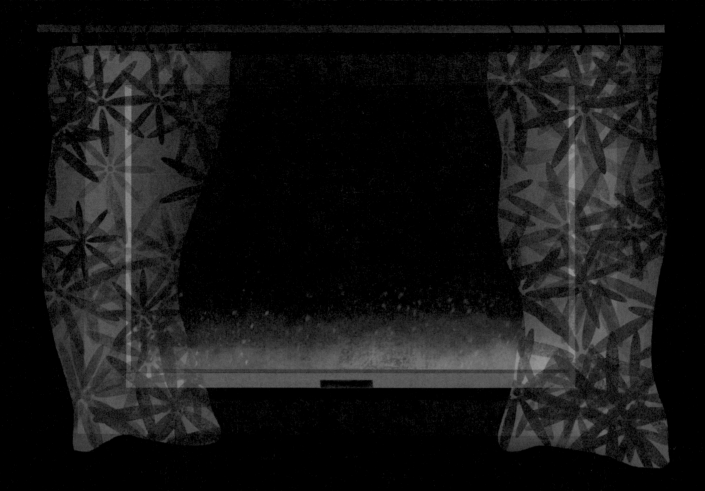

On Christmas Eve I went up to bed with a heavy heart. I had already decided that if Santa didn't leave me a present this year, then I probably didn't deserve one. I had left a letter for him on our kitchen windowsill weeks ago, but I was sure he would never give me what I'd asked him for. As I climbed under the sheets, the floor register near my bed blew tiny puffs of warm air up around my pillow. I pulled the blankets close to my chin to block out the cold and stared out the window. An empty night sky stared back at me, and I felt the little bit of hope I had left disappear. I curled up in the darkness, listening to the Christmas music that played on the transistor radio that Santa had brought me last Christmas. Finally, at eleven o'clock, they played the National Anthem and the radio station went off the air.

Sometime during the night, my sister poked me in the arm and said she was going downstairs to see if Santa had been to our house yet. It was still dark outside and I warned her not to go.

"What if he's down there?" I whispered. "What if he's down there *right now?*"

She didn't listen to me. I counted sixteen creaks on our stairs, then it was quiet. The next thing I heard were my sister's feet flying faster than I could count and her excited whispers saying over and over, "Get up! Get *up!* He was *here!*"

I will never forget how beautiful our Christmas tree looked all lit up in the dark of our living room that night. Silhouetted in colored lights, I could see bowls filled with roasted peanuts, tangerines, and ribbon candy tucked beneath the branches of our tree. A soft yellow glow lit up the nativity scene. I held my breath as I looked around the room, hoping there might be something for me. And then I saw it. The most beautiful guitar I had ever seen stood right beside the tree. I picked it up carefully. It wasn't a toy guitar like other kids had. It was a real guitar, like the kind my dad played! I could not believe that Santa had decided to give it to me.

The rest of the winter, everything went back to just the way it had been before. There was school, and homework, and chores, and life was just the same every day. But then one Saturday afternoon in late March, everything changed.

My sister and I were playing next to the house near the clothesline, where the snow had begun to melt in patches. Green grass was beginning to show up everywhere, and we rolled around on it, wishing it was summer. All of a sudden, I noticed something shiny poking out of the old snow under my mom's spirea bush.

"What's that?" I asked my sister.

"I don't know!" she snapped back, rolling her eyes.

I tried to climb under the bush, but there were so many branches in my way that I couldn't reach it. Thin, brittle twigs scratched my face and slush slid down the back of my neck, but I was not about to give up. I stretched my arm as far as I could and reached for it one more time. When I climbed out from under the bush, my sister held out her hand, expecting me to give her what I'd found.

"No way," I said, pulling it back.

I brushed the snow and ice away, and we both looked at it. I shook it and we both froze. *That sound.* I shook it again. *That sound! We'd heard it before! The night of our big fight in the kitchen!*

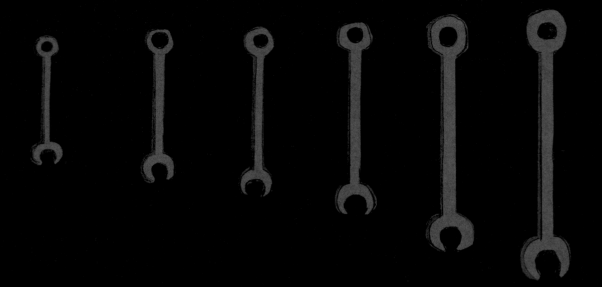

We both ran as fast as we could to the toolshed.

"Dad! Dad! Look what we found!" shouted my sister.

"Look what I found," I corrected her.

Our dad looked it over and said he had never seen a bell quite like that before. "There's a number eight printed on it," he said, pointing toward the top of the bell.

I quickly ran down the list in my head.

Dasher, Dancer, Prancer, Vixen,
Comet, Cupid, Donner, … BLITZEN!

I had found one of Blitzen's bells!

"Can I have it?" my sister asked him.

"Wait!" I said. "I'm the one who found it!"

My dad was silent for what seemed like nearly forever.

"Janet," he finally said, "you're the one who found it, so you can keep it."

The very next Monday, I took the bell to school to show some of my classmates. The one person I wanted to impress was not impressed at all.

"That looks like an old horse bell," she said with a smirk on her face.

"Well, we don't have horses on our farm, so explain that!"

She couldn't explain it and walked away without saying another word. The rest of my classmates looked the bell over carefully and decided I was one of the luckiest people they knew.

Later that day, at our afternoon recess, my unimpressed classmate marched up to me, looking triumphant.

"You know you can't keep it," she announced.

"Keep what?" I asked, narrowing my eyes and giving her the meanest look I knew how to give.

"The bell. If Santa really did lose it, then you have to give it back."

"No, I don't," I hissed. "My dad said I could keep it."

"Well, it's not your dad's bell, is it?"

Fighting back tears, I clenched my teeth together and said nothing. What could I say? As mad as she made me feel, I knew she was right. When she turned away, as bold and confident as ever, I pushed the sleigh bell deep into my coat pocket.

That night I climbed into our attic and put the sleigh bell in the old copper tub that held all of our Christmas decorations. At least for now, I thought, it's still mine.

The next Christmas, when my mom pulled
the lid off the copper tub, the bell was sitting right
where I'd left it. I held it in my hands, remembering
what my classmate had said to me. I knew I needed
to give the bell back to Santa.
So, on Christmas Eve, when we put out
the cookies and milk, I placed the bell on
the dining room table. I secretly hoped
Santa would leave it for me ... that
he wouldn't take it.

On Christmas morning, even before I looked under the tree, I ran to our dining room table. The cookies were gone, the glass of milk was empty ... but the bell was still there! A thin, gold ribbon was tied to the top of it now, and I held it up for my dad to see.

"I think he wants you to keep it," my dad said, smiling.

"I think he does, too," I said.

SOME CHILDREN GROW UP AND FORGET how it feels to be eleven years old. I have not forgotten. I remember how my heart ached for days over a mistake that could not be fixed. And I remember how a guitar, left beside a Christmas tree, was able to repair what could not be changed.

I'm not sure how old Santa is, but I think maybe he remembers how it feels to be eleven. And I'm guessing Santa knows what it's like to need a second chance.

A sled ride as Old Tom watches the fun!   Our new sheep Susie out for a summer walk.

Above left: The first day of school, waiting for bus #15 to pull into our driveway.

Above right: Christmas morning with my new REAL guitar!

Left: My family at Christmas.

JANET DEFEVER is a fourth-generation steward of her family's mid-Michigan farm, The Defever Homestead. Her love of nature and writing, combined with her experience as an MSU Advanced Master Gardener, were the beginning of the year-round children's programs that she hosts at The Homestead. *Second Chance Christmas* is her first children's book.

TAJÍN ROBLES is an artist living in Traverse City, Michigan. This is his third illustrated children's book. Find more of his work at TajinRobles.com.

Made in the USA
Middletown, DE
24 September 2022

10978724R00022